Humphrey's Garden

Sally Hunter

PUFFIN BOOKS

Humphrey's favourite thing...

is going ☀utside...

...into the garden.

Humphrey likes saying hello to
Molly, Mandy and Milly...

...looking for fairies...

...being a bit nosey... 🐝 ... 🐌

...talking to the big old tree...

...making a camp...

...pretending he can fly...

...finding a very secret place...

...picking the nicest flowers...

...and taking them home...